Other chapter books you might enjoy

The Amazing Trail of Seymour Snail

Lynn E. Hazen
Illustrated by Doug Cushman

Henry Holt and Company ★ New York

Many thanks to my talented critique buddies who laughed in all the right places; to Reka Simonsen for guiding Seymour on his path to publication; to Doug Cushman for bringing Seymour to humble and hilarious perfection; and to Jenny, Irma, and the preschool kids for reminding me to slow down, observe closely, and appreciate the slimy snail.

Henry Holt and Company, LLC
Publishers since 1866
175 Fifth Avenue
New York, New York 10010
www.HenryHoltKids.com

Henry Holt® is a registered trademark of Henry Holt and Company, LLC.
Text copyright © 2009 by Lynn E. Hazen
Illustrations copyright © 2009 by Doug Cushman
All rights reserved.
Distributed in Canada by H. B. Fenn and Company Ltd.

Library of Congress Cataloging-in-Publication Data
Hazen, Lynn E.
The amazing trail of Seymour Snail / by Lynn E. Hazen ;
illustrated by Doug Cushman.—1st ed.
p.   cm.
Summary: Hoping to become a famous artist one day, Seymour Snail
takes a job in a New York City art gallery, where everyone is buzzing
about a "magnificent mystery artist."
ISBN-13: 978-0-8050-8698-0 / ISBN-10: 0-8050-8698-6
[1. Snails—Fiction. 2. Artists—Fiction. 3. Art galleries, Commercial—
Fiction. 4. Insects—Fiction. 5. New York (N.Y.)—Fiction.] I. Cushman,
Doug, ill. II. Title.
PZ7.H314977Amc 2009   [E]—dc22   2008036939

First Edition—2009 / Designed by Véronique Lefèvre Sweet
Printed in April 2009 in the United States of America by Worzalla,
Stevens Point, Wisconsin, on acid-free paper. ∞

1 3 5 7 9 10 8 6 4 2

*Dedicated with love to my dad, who has
advised me all along to know my priorities,
to do what I have to do, and, no matter how
long it takes, to have fun along the way—
Thanks, Dad.*
—L. E. H.

⋆ Contents ⋆

★ 1 ★

Today's the Day

Seymour woke up in a happy mood. He took a puddle bath. He did his morning stretches, nibbled his leafy greens, and drank a bit of dew.

Seymour looked out his window. He felt inspired, so he painted a few pictures.

Then he checked his calendar. "Oh goody," said Seymour. "My friends are visiting today."

He looked around his leafy home. "Uh-oh," he said. "I'd better hide my paintings."

Seymour hoped to be a great artist someday. But he felt shy about showing his work.

So he hid his puddle paintings under the sofa. He stashed his leaf prints behind a lamp. But how could he hide his big mud sculptures?

"Hmm," said Seymour. "I have an idea!"

He covered one sculpture with a table-cloth and a pot of flowers. He covered the other one with a hat. Seymour oozed back to see how it looked.

"I hope no one notices," he said.

Ding dong.

"Wow," said Seymour. "My friends are here."

Seymour chatted with Roly Poly, Lady Bug, and Cricket. They had a lovely time until a big gust of wind blew in.

★ 2 ★

Whoosh!

*W*hoosh! The tablecloth lifted away. The hat blew off. Seymour's leaf prints and puddle paintings fluttered all over.

Oh no! What would his friends think?

Seymour's friends helped him gather
his artwork. They admired his lush green
leaf prints. They praised his dazzling
puddle paintings. And they pondered
his one-of-a-kind mud sculptures.

Seymour blushed. He wasn't used to so much attention.

"Wow," said Roly Poly. "I didn't know you were so creative. How long have you been making art?"

"All my life," Seymour whispered.

"Amazing," said Lady Bug. "You could get a job as an artist."

Seymour blushed again. "Gosh, do you really think so?"

"Absolutely," said Cricket. "Check for jobs in the newspaper."

"Good idea," said Seymour. "What could be better than a job as an artist?"

★ 3 ★

Looking for a Job

As soon as his friends left, he read every job in the Help Wanted section.

Seymour oozed to the phone booth and dialed. First he called Le Grand Burp, the famous French restaurant.

"Hello?" Seymour said. "I'm calling about the job in the newspaper."

"The menu designer's job has been filled," said the owner.

"Drat," said Seymour.

"We have a chef's job. Can you cook ze escargot?"

"Es-car-go?" Seymour asked.

"Oui. You can cook snails, yes?"

"No!"

Next, Seymour called the Gooey Garden Pest Control Company.

"I'm very creative with goo," said Seymour.

"Do you like to draw dead bugs with their feet pointed up to the sky?" asked the owner.

"Of course not," said Seymour. "Some of my best friends are bugs."

Click. The owner hung up on him.

How rude, Seymour thought.

★ 4 ★

Hard Work

"What's the matter, kid?" asked Mr. Earwig. He was waiting to use the phone.

"I want to be an artist," Seymour said. "But finding a job is hard work."

"The job market is very sluggish," said Mr. Earwig. "Especially for artists. Why don't you call my friend? He works at an art gallery. Here's his number." Mr. Earwig waited while Seymour made the call.

"Thank you," Seymour told Mr. Earwig, and he hung up the phone. "They want *me* to help out at the Speedy Arts Gallery. Isn't that perfect?"

"Good luck, kid," said Mr. Earwig.

"I'd better get going," said Seymour. "I start tomorrow. And it's a whole block away!"

★ 5 ★

Seymour Commutes
to Work

Seymour oozed through Central Park.
He listened to the happy hum of
insects. He wiggled his face in the
sweet-smelling flowers.

It was a glorious day.

He looped. He swayed. He twirled and turned. Then he glanced back at his sparkly trail and smiled. He liked the path he had taken and his own slimy designs.

Late in the afternoon, Seymour
stopped a moment to admire the warm
colors of the setting sun. "Beautiful, just
beautiful," he whispered, and he twirled
around and around.

As night fell, Seymour peeked at the perfect dewdrops glowing in the cool moonlight. He slimed onward, leaving a glittery trail behind him.

Just before dawn, Seymour zigzagged out of the park. He glided toward the Speedy Arts Gallery. Then he stuck himself onto a revolving door. *Whoosh!*

He stared in awe at the paintings in
the light-filled gallery. Seymour's eyeballs wiggled to and fro. "Wow," he said.
"Wow!"

"Snap out of it! Quit gawking!" yelled a grumpy green bug. Was this his new boss? Mr. Stink Bug tapped his stinky feet. "Hurry up! Follow me!"

"Yes, sir," said Seymour. He followed the grumpy bug into the gallery office.

⭐ 6 ⭐

Mr. Stink Bug

"Pay attention!" yelled Mr. Stink Bug. "Miss Spittle Bug quit right in the middle of sealing the invitations to next week's art show. So get to work. Slime all of these shut."

"Yes, sir," said Seymour.

Seymour was a little disappointed. Was this how he would spend his days at the art gallery? "Oh well," he said. "I guess even great artists have to start somewhere. I'll try my best."

Seymour was very good at sealing envelopes. He slimed shut mountains of mail! When he felt dry and puckery, a quick dip revived him.

But soon he was bored. Sealing envelopes was not very inspiring. He tried stacking them in amazing new ways. Nobody even noticed. Seymour closed his eyes. He thought about his leafy studio and all the creative projects he had left behind.

Mr. Stink Bug's angry voice jolted him out of his daydream. "No sleeping on the job! Deliver this priceless art to Coco La Roach on the second floor."

"Coco La Who?" asked Seymour.

"Coco La Roach. She's the gallery owner. Now get going!"

"Yes, sir." Seymour picked up the heavy package and headed to the stairs.

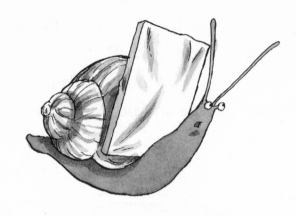

So Many Stairs

Yikes!

The stairwell was a scary place for a small snail with a bulky parcel.

The stairs seemed to go on and on forever.

Seymour slowly slimed his way up.

On the third step, he stopped for a rest. Everyone was rushing up and down the stairs, talking about a mysterious new artist.

"You should see the art," said a cute, hoppity grasshopper in high heels. "It's so inspiring. It makes me feel as if a fresh breeze is lifting my wings."

"Really?" said Seymour. He wanted to hear all about it. But—oh no!—his stinky boss was coming.

"Where have you been?" yelled Mr. Stink Bug. "Have you been dilly-dallying, shilly-shallying, and lolly-gagging on the job?"

"No," said Seymour. "I'm going as fast as I can."

"You're not fast enough! Get moving!"

Seymour slimed ever upward. On the fifth, sixth, and seventh steps, he overheard more about the dazzling new artist.

"Such glorious designs. What vision!"

"Perfect patterns. So full of heart."

Seymour wanted to stop. He wanted
to hear more about the mysterious art.
But he had three more steps to go.

Seymour could see the water cooler at
the top of the stairs. He longed for a sip.

★ 8 ★

Mr. Stink Bug—Again!

Seymour struggled on.

Then he bumped into Mr. Stink Bug again.

"What's taking you so long? If you don't deliver my package to Coco La Roach by five o'clock, you're FIRED!"

Uh-oh, Seymour thought.

Maybe working at the Speedy Arts Gallery wasn't the perfect job after all. But Seymour kept going.

"Hey, kid!" said a spider, when Seymour had just one step to go. "Didn't anyone tell you about the elevator?"

"The elevator?" asked a very tired Seymour.

"Yep," the spider said. "It's a wonderful high-speed invention."

Seymour thanked him for pointing it out.

"Glad to help," said the spider. He handed Seymour his card. "Look me up sometime. I'm onto something big. It's called the World Wide Web."

Seymour wanted to talk to the friendly spider, but time was running out. Seymour finally made it to the water cooler. He was so thirsty! But he didn't have time to stop.

He hurried down the hall.

At last he reached Coco La Roach's door. Seymour was about to knock when the door swung open.

Coco leaped right over him! "Moe!" she shouted. "Have you found that mystery artist yet?"

★ 9 ★

Five Minutes
After Five O'clock

"Wait!" Seymour pleaded, but everyone ignored him. Seymour was nearly squashed. And now the grumpy Mr. Stink Bug was skittering toward him.

"It's five minutes after five o'clock! And you *still* haven't delivered my package?" Mr. Stink Bug shouted. "You're FIRED!"

A swarm of fireflies flew out of Mr. Stink Bug's briefcase. "Fired! Fired! Fired!" they screamed at Seymour.

Seymour blinked back tears. *I'm just no good at anything,* he thought. Still he nudged the package toward Coco's fancy shoes.

"What's this?" Coco asked.

"It's for you," whispered Seymour. He turned around and tried to sneak away.

"Yuck!" said Coco. "It's another paint-by-numbers delivery from that awful stinkbug." She tossed the package into the trash. "I told him five times already. No more of his ridiculous self-portraits in my gallery."

"All those stairs for nothing," Seymour sighed.

Coco gazed out her big window. "Why is everyone standing around? Moe, keep looking for the mystery artist!"

Mystery artist? Seymour thought. *I wonder who that could be?*

⋆10⋆

The View

Seymour was curious. He just had to find out. He slimed and swirled across the floor. *Maybe I can sneak a peek,* Seymour thought. He took a round-about path so no one could see him.

He inched closer and closer to the huge window.

"Isn't the art in the park amazing?" Coco said.

"Breathtaking," said Moe.

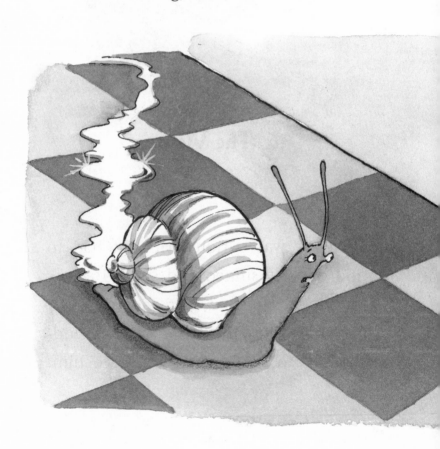

Seymour looked out the window. Seymour couldn't believe his eyeballs. He saw a spectacular view of Central Park. Crowds of art lovers were taking photos.

"Dazzling," said Coco. "Look how it glimmers in the afternoon sunlight. But who is the artist?"

"It's me," Seymour gasped. "Me!"

"YOU?" shouted Coco La Roach. "Hold it right there!"

★ 11 ★

Uh-oh!

"Uh-oh," said Seymour. He gulped and pulled into his shell as fast as he could. Maybe he'd *never* come out again. He hoped Coco didn't know any French chefs.

Coco stared at Seymour's slime on her office floor. She looked out her window at the art in the park, and she compared the glimmering trails.

"It *is* you!" she raved. "You're the magnificent mystery artist!"

"Gosh," said Seymour. He blushed and peeked out of his shell. "Do you like my art? Really?"

Coco and Moe nodded.

"Your designs are so amazing," said Coco. "Simply superb."

"How do you do it?" asked Moe.

Seymour perked up. "It just oozes out of me," he said. "And I have been practicing all my life."

"Fantastic," said Moe. "But look! Your masterpiece is fading away."

Seymour smiled. "I can always make more."

★ 12 ★

Seymour, the World–Famous Artist

At last everyone knew that Seymour was a great artist.

He kept busy making all kinds of unusual art. His magnificent creations were even featured in *Bug Art* Magazine and *The New York Slimes*. Seymour was a

little surprised at the wonder of it all.
But his good friends Cricket, Lady Bug,
and Roly Poly were not surprised at all.
They were his biggest fans.

"We knew you could do it, Seymour!" they told him.

"Gosh, thanks," said Seymour. "I'm just doing what I like to do."

Soon Seymour was traveling far and wide, enjoying what he did best: oozing along at a snail's pace and leaving his own glittery mark on the world.